PON

**DO NOT REMOVE
CARDS FROM POCKET**

A Break-of-Day Book

Ever since 1928, when Wanda Gág's classic *Millions of Cats* appeared, Coward-McCann has been publishing books of high quality for young readers. Among them are the easy-to-read stories known as Break-of-Day books. This series appears under the colophon shown above — a rooster crowing in the sunrise — which is adapted from one of Wanda Gág's illustrations for *Tales from Grimm*.

Though the language used in Break-of-Day books is deliberately kept as clear and as simple as possible, the stories are not written in a controlled vocabulary. And while chosen to be within the grasp of readers in the primary grades, their content is far-ranging and varied enough to captivate children who have just begun crossing the momentous threshold into the world of books.

Nate the Great
STALKS
STUPIDWEED

by Marjorie Weinman Sharmat

illustrated by Marc Simont

Coward-McCann Inc. New York

Text copyright © 1986 by Marjorie Weinman Sharmat
Illustrations copyright © 1986 by Marc Simont
All rights reserved. This book, or parts thereof,
may not be reproduced in any form without permission
in writing from the publishers. Published simultaneously
in Canada by General Publishing Co. Limited, Toronto.
First impression
Printed in the United States of America

Library of Congress Cataloging-in-Publication Data
Sharmat, Marjorie Weinman.
Nate the Great stalks stupidweed.
Summary: Nate the Great searches for a missing weed
after it disappears from a pot on Oliver's porch.
[1. Weeds—Fiction.   2. Mystery and
detective stories]   I. Title.
PZ7.S5299Nax   1986   [E]   85-30161
ISBN 0-698-20626-6

To my son Andrew,
who I'm sure would have given me
his enormously helpful suggestions
even if I didn't do his laundry

I, Nate the great detective,

was weeding my garden.

My dog Sludge was digging in it.

Oliver came over.

Oliver always comes over.

Oliver is a pest.

"I have just lost a weed," he said.

"No problem," I said.

"You may have all of mine."

"But this was *my* weed,"

Oliver said. "Can you help me

find it?"

"I, Nate the Great, am not going
to look for a weed.
I only take important cases."
"This is an important weed,"
Oliver said. "I bought it
for a nickel at Rosamond's
ADOPT-A-WEED sale.

Rosamond picks weeds
that nobody wants
and she finds homes for them."
"I believe it," I said.
"She gave me a Certificate of Ownership,"
Oliver said. He pointed to something
sticking out of his back pocket.
It was a thick, rolled-up
piece of paper
with a ribbon tied around it.
Oliver pulled the paper
out of his pocket
and handed it to me.
I untied the ribbon
and unrolled the paper.

It was long.

It had printing on it.

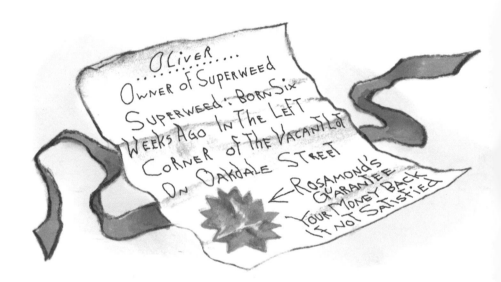

Oliver. . . . .
Owner of Superweed
Superweed: Born Six
Weeks Ago In The Left
Corner of The Vacant Lot
On Oakdale Street
← Rosamond's
Guarantee
Your Money Back
If Not Satisfied

There was a shiny seal
stuck on the paper.
It also had printing on it.

"See? It's an important weed,"
Oliver said. "It also came with
a record that Rosamond made
to play to her weeds
to help them grow.
Be proud you're a weed,
wild and free,
and you might grow up
to be a tree."
"Rosamond thinks big," I said,
"as well as strange."
I gave the Certificate of Ownership
back to Oliver.
He put it in his pocket.

"Tell me," I said,
"what happened after you
bought the weed?"
"I took it home,"
Oliver said. "But it looked sick.
I played Rosamond's record for it.
Then it looked sicker.
So I went to the library
and found a big book about weeds.
I took it home.
I read about sick weeds
and healthy weeds.
The book told me how
to make sick weeds healthy.
It gave three steps.
Step One. *Put the weed in dirt*.

12

I got a pot with dirt in it.

Then I stuck the weed in it.

Step Two. *Give the weed sun.*

I took the weed in the pot

out to my back porch

and put it on my railing

where the sun was shining.

Step Three. *Give the weed water*.

I went into the house

for a glass of water.

When I got back to the porch

with the water,

the pot was there,

but the weed was gone."

"Perhaps the weed did not like

what you were doing to it,"

I said. "Perhaps it escaped."

"I never did the third step,"

Oliver said.

"I have already solved your case,"
I said.
"Today is a breezy day.
The weed blew away in the breeze.
The breeze is going east.
Your weed could be in China by now."
"But China is way outside my porch,"
Oliver said.
"And my porch is screened in."
"I, Nate the Great,
do not want to look for your weed," I said.
"I would not know it
if I found it."
"My weed looks small and scraggly and sick,"
Oliver said.
"It has a yellow bud.

Rosamond said it will grow

into a flower

that will reach

as high as the sky.

That is why I bought it."

Oliver stood there

and looked up at the sky.

He might stay forever

if I did not look for his weed.

"Very well," I said.

"I will take your case."

I wrote a note to my mother.

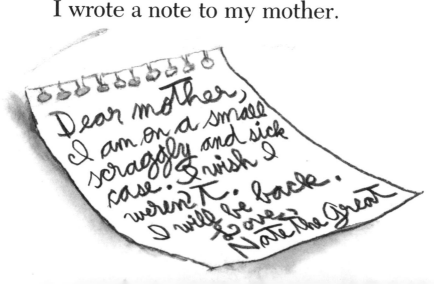

Dear mother,
I am on a small
scraggly and sick
case. I wish I
weren't. I will be back.
Love,
Nate the Great

"Show me where your weed disappeared,"
I said to Oliver.

Oliver, Sludge and I walked to
Oliver's back porch.

It was screened in.

I looked for holes and cracks.

But I could not find any.

I looked at the railing.

It was covered with dirt.

A pot of dirt was sitting on it.

Beside the pot was a big book.

With a dirty fingerprint on the cover.

But I could read the cover.

It said *Wonderful Weeds of the World*.

Wonderful
Weeds of the
World

I walked around the porch.

I looked in corners,

and under and on top of things.

Sludge sniffed.

"Your weed has to be

on this porch," I said.

"But it isn't here.

This is a tough case.

I must go to Rosamond's

ADOPT-A-WEED sale.

Perhaps I will learn something there."

"I will follow you," Oliver said.

"Not if I can help it," I said.

I, Nate the Great, and Sludge

ran to Rosamond's house.

She was sitting outside

behind a table

that was covered with weeds and cats.

There was a big can of water

under the table.

There was a sign beside the table.

"I am looking for Oliver's lost weed,"
I said.

"He lost his weed?" Rosamond asked.

"That was my star weed.

It will grow to the sky.

It's Superweed."

"It's sick," I said.

"Oliver didn't love it enough,"
Rosamond said.

"Would you know it
if you saw it again?" I asked.

"I know all my weeds,"
Rosamond said. "I keep a list
of them in this book."

Rosamond opened a book
she had on her lap.

21

"Oliver's weed has a yellow bud,"
she said.
"I already know that," I said.
"And its name is Superweed,"
Rosamond said.
"I know that, too."
I, Nate the Great, had a
better name for it.
But I did not think that
Rosamond would like
Stupidweed.
"You have told me everything
I already knew," I said.
"Oh, good," Rosamond said.
"I knew I could help you."
Rosamond closed her book.

Annie and her dog Fang
were coming down the street.
Sludge ducked under the table.
He knocked over the can of water.
It fell on Rosamond's feet.
PLOP!

"Sloppy Sludge!" Rosamond cried.

"You got my feet wet!"

This was not a good day for Sludge.

He was afraid of Fang.

He was also afraid of Rosamond's cats.

I spoke to Annie.

"I am looking for a weed
with a yellow bud on it."
"Maybe Fang ate it," Annie said.
"Is Fang a weed eater?" I asked.
"Fang will eat almost everything,"
Annie said. "Watch!"
Annie shouted, "Fang! WEED!"
Fang grabbed a weed in his teeth
and started to run away.
"You owe me two cents, Fang!"
Rosamond shouted.
Rosamond's four cats ran after Fang.
I hoped that Fang and the cats
would have a big fight.
I hoped they would all lose.
The world would be safe forever.

Sludge ran out

from under the table.

He knew it was time to leave.

We had to look for Stupidweed.

But where?

Perhaps we should look where

lots of things grow.

Perhaps we could find a clue

in the woods

or in a park.

Sludge and I walked to the woods.

We peered inside.

It was dark and scary in there.

It was almost as scary as Fang.

I, Nate the Great, hate cases

where I have to be brave.

Sludge and I crawled into the woods.

We heard something behind us.

It was gaining on us.

It was Oliver.

Sludge and I hid behind a tall tree.

Oliver ran into the woods.

Sludge and I ran out.

We ran to the park.

We sat down on a bench.

Everything was sunny and bright.

And safe.

I liked it there.

Flowers and plants were everywhere.

Was there a clue among

all these growing things?

Was there a weed?

Suddenly I saw something.

It was Claude.

Claude is always losing things.

He was crawling down a path

among the flowers.

"Did you lose something?" I asked.

"A worm," he said. "It crawled

into the ground.

I can't see it

but I know it is in there.

It is right under our noses.

Can you help me find it?"

This was not a good day for

me, Nate the Great.

I had been asked to find a weed.

I had been asked to find a worm.

It was time to do something

important.

I went home and made pancakes.

I gave Sludge a bone.

I thought about the case.

I had to find the weed

and lose Oliver.

But I was stumped.

The weed could not have left

Oliver's porch.

But it was not there.

I thought about clues.

What had I learned?

The weed's name is Superweed.

I knew that was not important.

The weed has a yellow bud.

Maybe that was important.

Maybe it wasn't.

The weed was last seen inside a pot

on Oliver's railing.

Last seen is always important.

What was Oliver doing

just before the weed disappeared?

He was reading from a book

and looking at his weed

and turning away from his weed

to go into his house.

Werc *those* clues?

I thought of Rosamond.

She was strange.

That was not a clue.

That was her problem.

Then I thought about her book

and her can of water.

Hmm.

I looked at Sludge

eating his bone.

He always tries to help with my cases.

But all he had done was knock over

Rosamond's can of water.

Was he trying to tell me something?

I thought about Claude
and his worm.
Suddenly I knew I had
a lot of good clues.
I had to go back to Oliver's house.
It was hard to do.

Oliver was sitting on his back porch.

"I lost you in the woods," he said.

"Did you find my weed?"

"I am getting close," I said.

I looked at his railing.

"Where is your weed book?"

"I took it back to the library,"
Oliver said.

"Then I, Nate the Great, must go
to the library."

"I will follow you," Oliver said.

"I know it," I said.

Sludge and I rushed to the library.

Sludge had to wait outside.

I went inside.

I looked for weed books.

I found *Wonderful Weeds of the World*.

It had a dirty fingerprint

on the cover

so I knew it was Oliver's copy.

I pulled it down.

I opened it up.

I looked inside.

I found what I knew I would find.

Oliver's weed!

It was between two pages.

It was pressed against

Step Three.

It did not look sick anymore.

It looked dead.

I took the weed from the book
and put the book
back on the shelf.
I knew that Steps One, Two
and Three could not help
Oliver's weed.
Nothing could help Oliver's weed.
I left the library.
Oliver was outside with Sludge.
I held up the weed
with both hands.
It needed both hands
to keep it up.
"Here is your weed," I said.
"The case is solved."
"How did you find it?" Oliver asked.

"Clues," I said. "Lots of clues.
I saw Claude looking for a worm
in the ground.
He said he could not see it

but he knew it was in there

just under our noses.

I thought about that.

Your weed could have been *in*

something close by

but we still could not see it.

What was near the pot?

What was just under our noses?

Your weed book!

But you gave me the biggest clue

when you said you were using the book

when the weed disappeared.

When I saw your book,

it was closed.

I remember reading the title

on the cover.

It had to be closed
for me to do that.
But it should have been open
because you were still using it.
Rosamond closed *her* book
when she was *through* with it.
Why was your book closed
when you *weren't* through with it?"
Oliver shrugged.
"I, Nate the Great, will tell you why.
The breeze blew it closed
while you were getting the water."
"So what?" Oliver said.
"*After* the weed fell into it!" I said.
"What?" Oliver gasped. "Why would
the weed do that?"

"Because it was hit by the
Certificate of Ownership
sticking out of your back pocket.
When you turned to go into your house,
the certificate hit the weed,
and the weed fell into the book.
PLOP!
Just like Rosamond's can of water
fell over when Sludge hit it.

Turn your back to the pot, Oliver."

Oliver turned.

"Aha! Your certificate is aimed

directly at the pot. Perfect aim."

"I wasn't trying," Oliver said.

"Your weed was sick," I said.

"It was in dry dirt.

It was easy for it to plop.

It was right under our noses.

But we couldn't see it.

Just like Claude and his worm."

"So my weed didn't go to China,"

Oliver said.

"I, Nate the Great,

make a few mistakes."

Oliver stared at his weed.

"This weed looks terrible.

It will never reach the sky.

I am going to Rosamond's house

to get my nickel back."

"I am going home," I said.

I said good-bye to Oliver.

I liked doing that.

"I will be over later," he said.

"I know it," I said.

Sludge and I went back to our garden.

I started to weed again.

But I was tired of weeds.

Perhaps Rosamond could come over

and pick them all.

She would give them names

and homes.

That would make everybody happy.

Especially me.

I had better things to do.
I, Nate the Great, went back
to the library
and took out
a good, clean book.